For perplexed parents everywhere - C.C.

Mantra Lingua
5 Alexandra Grove, London N12 8NU
www.mantralingua.com

有個嗚嗚咽咽的嬰兒，
我們怎麼辦？

What Shall We Do With The **BOO HOO BABY?**

by Cressida Cowell

Illustrated by Ingrid Godon

Chinese translation by Sylvia Denham

Mantra Lingua

嬰兒說:

The baby said,

「嗚..嗚..咽..咽..！」

"Boo-hoo-hoo!"

「嘎嘎？」
鴨子說。

"Quack?"
said the duck.

有個嗚嗚咽咽的嬰兒，
我們怎麼辦？

What shall we do with
the boo-hoo baby?

「餵他呀，」小狗說道。

"Feed him," said the dog.

於是牠們便餵嬰兒。

So they fed the baby.

「喵喵！」
貓兒叫道，

"Miaow!"
said the cat.

「汪汪！」
小狗叫道，

"Bow-wow!"
said the dog.

「嘎嘎！」
鴨子叫道，

"Quack!"
said the duck.

「哞哞！」
母牛叫道，

"Moo!"
said the cow,

跟著...

and...

「嗚..嗚..咽..咽..！」
嬰兒哭著叫。

"Boo-hoo-hoo!"
said the baby.

有個嗚嗚咽咽的嬰兒，
我們怎麼辦？
「給他洗澡呀，」
貓兒說道。

What shall we do with
the boo-hoo baby?
"Bath him,"
said the cat.

於是牠們便給嬰兒洗澡。

So they bathed the baby.

「嘎嘎！」
鴨子叫道，

"Quack!"
said the duck.

「汪汪！」
小狗叫道，

"Bow-wow!"
said the dog.

「喵喵！」
貓兒叫道，

"Miaow!"
said the cat.

「嗚..嗚..咽..咽..！」
嬰兒哭著叫。

"Boo-hoo-hoo!"
said the baby.

有個嗚嗚咽咽的嬰兒，
我們怎麼辦？
「跟他玩呀，」
母牛說道。

What shall we do with
the boo-hoo baby?
"Play with him,"
said the cow.

於是牠們便跟嬰兒玩。

So they played with the baby.

「喵喵！」
貓兒叫道，

"Miaow!"
said the cat.

「汪汪！」
小狗叫道，

"Bow-wow!"
said the dog.

「嘎嘎！」
鴨子叫道，

"Quack!"
said the duck.

「哞哞！」
母牛叫道，

"Moo!"
said the cow,

跟著…

and...

「嗚..嗚..咽..咽..！」
嬰兒哭著叫。

"Boo-hoo-hoo!"
said the baby.

有個嗚嗚咽咽的嬰兒，
我們怎麼辦？
「放他到床上去呀，」
鴨子說道。

What shall we do with
the boo-hoo baby?
"Put him to bed,"
said the duck.

So they put him to bed

「喵喵！」
貓兒叫道，

"Miaow!"
said the cat.

於是牠們便將嬰兒放到床上去。

「汪汪！」
小狗叫道，

「嘎嘎！」
鴨子叫道，

「哞哞！」
母牛叫道，

"Bow-wow!"
said the dog.

"Quack!"
said the duck.

"Moo!"
said the cow,

跟著…

and…

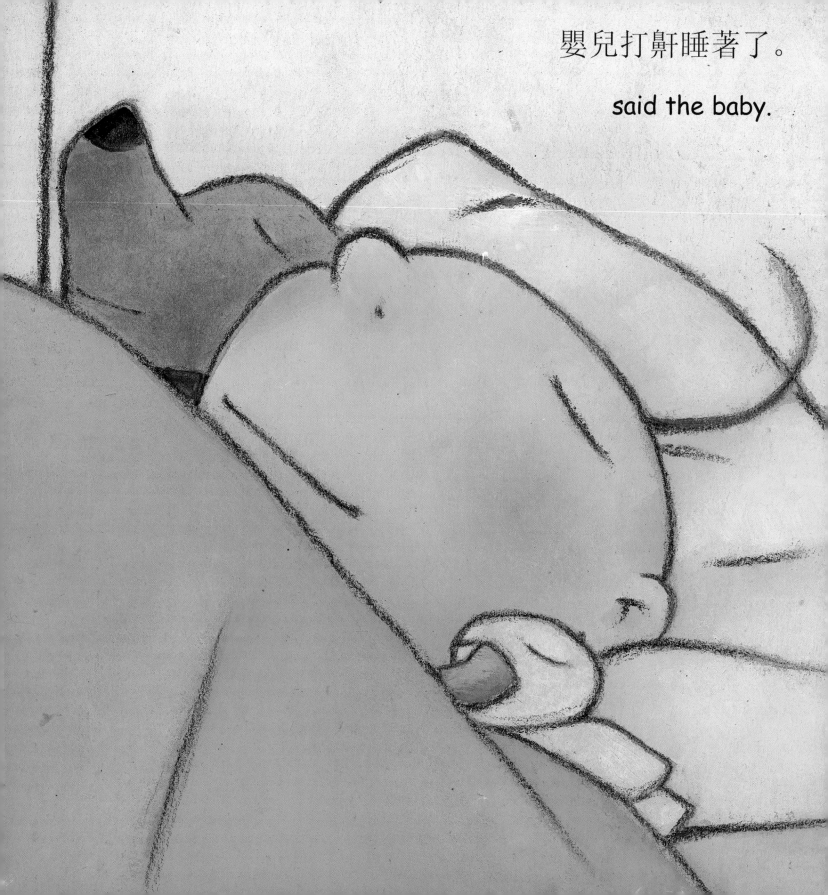

嬰兒打鼾睡著了。

said the baby.